THE BEGINNING
OF THE END
- OF OUR CIVILIZATION

Jorn Heldrup
132, Stenlokken
3460 Birkerod
Danmark
Cell: +45 51 23 82 47
heldrupj@dadlnet.dk

Copyright © Jorn Heldrup and MyLifeTree Publisher, Copenhagen, September 2021

Cover Photo: Jorn Heldrup (Playa Sámara, Costa Rica)

ISBN 978-87-971594-1-5

"For Tania, Ea and Gry and the newly born children of the world."

Preface

We have all collectively boarded Titanic, but contrary to the passengers in April 1912, we now know that the Titanic will encounter several devastating events in the coming years and decades. The children born today have no responsibility for the global warming we are currently experiencing. Still, they will be the first generation to be subjected to the consequences of our collective inaction. The music is playing on Titanic, and we are behaving more or less as we have always done and not recognizing the results of our inaction. This novel attempts to describe what could happen if we continue to behave like we are today. It is the hope that this novel will contribute to getting decision-makers, whether in Government or industry, and human beings worldwide to take climate change much more seriously and accelerate the efforts to reduce CO_2 emissions. And thereby seek to prevent the worst effects of the ongoing climate changes.

The international organizations established after World War II are already struggling to address the current emergencies in the world. With the evolving refugee situation and increased poverty, conflicts, hunger, freshwater shortages, warming, wildfires, rapidly spreading infectious diseases, and other disasters in the world, international organizations will face increasing challenges in handling the consequences of global warming in the coming decades. We have a window of opportunity to allow our children and grandchildren to live in a world with diminished effects of global warming, but that window is getting closer to closing every day; we pretend that the icebergs are not there on the horizon.

The Covid-19 pandemic was a potent warning that humanity's tampering with nature could have severe consequences and that the most severe threat to civilization in the form of global warming has yet to be addressed. The difference between the pandemic and the climate crisis is that vaccines cannot control the latter. The consequences of inaction will make the coronavirus crisis look like a poorly planned dress rehearsal for what is to come in the coming decades. It is up to each one of us to do what we can to allow our children and grandchildren to live their life in a world where their basic needs are met and where they can pursue a life in line with their aspirations.

Chapter 1

Sandy

Lara was born in London by the end of the 2000s. Her parents were from Denmark and the United States, respectively, and she grew up in different countries where her parents had worked during her childhood. In many ways, she represented the children who grew up in the globalized world at the time, and during her years in international schools, she had made friends with children and young adults from all over the world.

During her childhood, her parents had often discussed global warming and the associated climate changes with their friends and visitors from all corners of the globe. Her parents had many books on global warming, and Lara clearly remembered a white cover book with a picture taken of Africa, the Middle East, and Antarctica at the halfway point between the

Moon and Earth. It illustrated the spectacularly beautiful Earth, unique in the solar system and possibly unique in the Universe.

One of Lara's earliest childhood memories was a visit to her grandparents in New York City in late 2012. Lara and her mother, Carole, arrived in New York at the end of October. Her grandparents lived in Brooklyn Heights in a large apartment overlooking the Manhattan skyline and East River. Lara loved to visit her grandparents and was keen to go to the playgrounds next to Brooklyn Heights Promenade. Her grandparents had told them about Hurricane Sandy, which claimed many lives in the Caribbean and some deaths on the East Coast of the United States. It was very unusual to have hurricanes reaching as far north as New Jersey and New York. But since the water on the East Cost was unusually warm that year, it allowed the hurricane to gain strength and size. When it hit New York, it was one of the largest storm systems ever recorded in this part of the United States, stretching more than 1,600 kilometers. The wind was not particularly strong when Sandy hit New York, but the storm surge and the slow-moving storm which dumped vast amounts of water made the difference. The sea level on the East Coast had risen around 30 centimeters over the last hundred years, contributing to the storm surge that led to severe flooding of lower Manhattan and low-lying areas of Queens, Brooklyn, and Staten Island. Besides the tragic death of approximately 230 people in its path, it was estimated that Sandy led to damages in the United States of roughly 65 billion USD, making it the second most costly storm in US history at the time.

Lara remembered the preparations for the storm and how they had purchased extra water and food supplies for themselves. Supermarkets in Brooklyn Heights were close to being out of stock of all essential supplies since traffic in and out of the city had been stopped by the authorities before the arrival of the hurricane. By noon, the streets were almost empty, and people were heading home to avoid the worst effects of the storm. Lara's family gathered for an early dinner in anticipation of potential power cuts related to the hurricane. Her mother read her a story before bedtime, and the whole family went to bed early, fearing the possible damages to their apartment, building complex, and the neighborhood.

The following day was surreal given the extensive flooding and blackout of the whole Southern part of Manhattan. People were standing in long lines to receive clean bottled water, and the subway system, train stations, and airports were closed for several days, and even the stock exchange was shut down. The local schools closed for a week, and Lara and Carole had to stay with Lara's grandparents for an additional week until the airports opened and could accommodate all the visitors stranded in New York City. Lara enjoyed the extra days with her grandparents, but Carole had to reschedule meetings related to her work. Later, it was estimated that Sandy had been the most damaging storm to hit New York City area since around 1700 AD.

Dar es Salaam

Tanzania was at the time a fast-growing country with a population of around 45 million, with Dar es Salaam being the largest city and the commercial hub with about 4 million people. Traffic was getting more and more congested since the infrastructure could not keep up with the fast-growing population and the rapid economic growth. The city was located on the Indian Ocean. It had a thieving harbor and a traffic and rail hub for the roads and railway lines leading into the relatively large country.

Lara grew up in Dar es Salaam with her parents. Her father was employed by the World Bank, and her mother worked for a big international telecommunication company.

Their house was situated just north of the city center on the Northern tip of the Msasani peninsula. The Masaki area had been transformed from a sleepy, laid-back residential area to a high-class residential and tourist area within a relatively short time. Lara was cared for by a local Yaya (nanny) during her early childhood years while her parents were at work. The afternoons were spent on the beach at the nearby Yacht Club, where families enjoyed the tree-covered beach and engaged in all sorts of water sports in the secluded Msasani Bay.

Lara was an easygoing and self-confident child who never doubted that her parents loved her. She was energetic, optimistic, curious, and extroverted and quickly made friends with the other children on the beach. Her parents often traveled in their respective jobs, but they had a rule that they would not both be away from Dar es Salaam while Lara was a young child. She started in the local kindergarten at the age of three and enjoyed the many new activities there. She was taken to the kindergarten by her Yaya in the morning and brought back home after lunch. Her parents had employed a cook, a gardener, and a house aid to take care of the small family, and the house was guarded by a local security company 24/7.

Lara clearly remembered the family holidays in Tanzania, where they visited many of the famous national parks in the country. One thing was to see and hear about the wildlife in Africa from children's books but having the opportunity as a young child to experience the wildlife in their natural habitat was an extraordinary experience. The memories of the vast savannah with big herds of wildebeest, zebras, buffalos, and groups of giraffes and elephants were inscribed in Lara's brain for the rest of her life, including the sense of being in a place where the wildlife and nature dominated everything around her.

Irma

Lara enjoyed her holidays as a child with her parents and grandparents, and one of her favorite places was her grandparents' cottage on St. John in the US Virgin Islands. Her grandparents spent more and more of their time on the island away from the cold winter months in the northeastern United States. Her grandparents had previously used their cottage in Florida during the winter months but found that the setting and warmer weather on St. John was ideal for the kind of life they were looking for during their winter holidays. Lara's parents would try to visit St. John at least once a year, and over the years, Lara got to know the island well with its lush vegetation, secluded beaches, and rich marine life.

The cottage was situated on the ridge which ran from the east to the west on the small island. The view from the house was magnificent, with the British Virgin Islands to the north of the cottage and the Coral Bay with all the yachts to the south.

All this changed in September 2017 when the US Virgin Islands, including St. John and St. Thomas, took a direct hit by the category 5 Hurricane Irma. It was the most devastating natural disaster the two islands had experienced, and it caused considerable structural damage to buildings and infrastructure. Luckily, Lara's grandparents were not on the island at the time, but their cottage was severely damaged. It made a big impression on Lara to see the photos of the damaged cottage and learn that hurricanes were getting more potent and more destructive because of the global warming associated with the increasing CO_2 and methane in the atmosphere. She also knew that it was becoming more and more expensive to insure a cottage on the islands, which meant that many people, including her grandparents, had canceled their insurance policies and had to cover all costs associated with the reconstruction of their cottage.

Fortunately, her grandparents retained their small condo on the west coast of Florida just south of Tampa and could use the condo again after having rented it out for quite some time. The residents on the Islands were in a very different situation, with many homes being uninhabitable and repair costs that would exceed the savings of many families. Many had jobs related to the tourist industry, which had taken considerable time to recover after the hurricane.

Geneva

Lara moved with her parents to Geneva just before she started in 1st grade at the International School of Geneva. Her campus was on a plateau on the Northern side of Lake Geneva with a magnificent view of the western part of the lake and the Alps, dominated by Mont Blanc, the highest mountain in Europe.

Geneva was home to numerous United Nations Agencies and Organizations, which brought people from all over the world to the city and the surrounding suburbs in Switzerland and the bordering French municipalities. Private for-profit and non-profit companies and organizations were also increasingly placing their regional or international headquarters in the Francophone cantons around Geneva.

All this meant that the area attracted people from all corners of the world and gave it a distinctly international atmosphere. It also meant that Lara's school had students from close to 100 countries who benefitted from the interaction with children from different cultures, religions, and ethnic groups. Given its location, prestige, and benefits packages, it was also possible to attract some of the world's best and most qualified teachers.

Lara loved the school, made many new friends, and was fascinated by the many new subjects introduced in the primary school. Lara was on a bilingual program where the teaching was in both English and French so that by the end of primary school, the students were completely bilingual.

Lara's parents continued to work for their respective organizations but were increasingly involved in the international efforts to address the causes and consequences of global warming. They bought a house close to Lara's school so that she could easily ride her bicycle to the school and visit friends in the neighborhood.

Lara considered Geneva her hometown and always looked back on her time in the area as a defining experience that changed the rest of her life. She lived in Geneva for 13 years until she finished her International Baccalaureate

Diploma Program. Her life revolved around school, friends, and downtown Geneva. She also enjoyed the many vacation and recreation opportunities in the area, with hikes in the mountains during the spring, summer, and autumn months and skiing in the winter. She had a core group of close female friends and had her first love affair as a teenager. Over the years, she focused on subjects relating to geography, nature, global warming, and development, which was accentuated by a summer camp experience in the Southern part of India.

Lara had developed into a very gifted and compassionate person, with highly developed social skills, which allowed her to communicate and associate with people of all ages and different walks of life. She had an inner compass based on clear ethical and moral believes. Lara was very observant, listened attentively to her peers, and had a positive and constructive approach to all challenges and tasks in her life. Her family had dogs throughout her childhood, and it was apparent that any pet or animal she encountered sensed her caring and loving nature.

Wuhan

In late December 2019, a young Chinese doctor at Wuhan Union Hospital in Central China shared information with his colleagues at another Wuhan hospital about a possible outbreak of SARS in the city. His concern was based on data from the Wuhan Centre for Disease Control and an internal report at his hospital concerning a suspected SARS patient. The Wuhan police later questioned the medical doctor and accused him of spreading false information about an unconfirmed disease outbreak. Within few months, the new SARS virus had spread to all corners of the world and led to the most severe pandemic since the 1918 Spanish flu. The Chinese doctor himself contracted Coronavirus disease

(COVID-19), the infectious disease caused by severe acute respiratory syndrome coronavirus 2 (SARS-CoV-2), in early 2020 and died of complications to the disease.

For years, infectious diseases specialists had warned health officials and politicians that new contagious diseases would emerge at an increasing rate given the higher rate of trade in exotic animals and the widespread intrusion of modern agriculture into rainforests. The transfer of the simian immunodeficiency virus 'SIV' from monkeys to humans in the form of the human immunodeficiency virus 'HIV' and the Ebola virus from bats to humans in Africa were early warnings of what was to come. The world was poorly prepared for the COVID-19 pandemic. It took many months for most countries' health officials and politicians to understand that the pandemic would severely affect the health systems, societies, and economies and lead to the worst economic crisis since the great depression in the 1920s.

The virus challenged the political and economic fabric of the world and exposed significant challenges in globalization. National states and many states in the Unions of states took control of their societies to fight the new virus. The lack of preparedness made many countries revisit their emergency plans and build strategic protective supplies and equipment stockpiles. New effective vaccines against the virus were developed, tested, and released in record time as the only effective measure to control the disease in the medium to long term. Billions of vaccines were produced and distributed to all corners of the world. The numerous people and interest groups skeptical of the value of modern vaccines kept a relatively low profile during the rollout of the vaccines.

The pandemic was a potent warning to the world that humanity's tampering with nature could have severe consequences and that the most severe threat to civilization in the form of global warming had yet to be addressed. The difference between the pandemic and the climate crisis was that a vaccine could not control the latter. The consequences of inaction would make the coronavirus crisis look like a poorly planned dress rehearsal.

Greenland

Her father invited Lara to join him on a trip to Greenland after graduating from the International School in Geneva. They spent the first week in Copenhagen, where they visited Lars' two children from his first marriage. Lara had difficulty imagining that her father had lived in Copenhagen before she was born and had two children from his first marriage. But she loved her Danish brother and sister, and being an only child; she appreciated having an extended family in Denmark. Katja was in her last year of her master's program at the University of Copenhagen. Kasper had started working for one of the government ministries in

Copenhagen. She had many conversations with them about her thoughts concerning what to study in the coming years.

Lars and Lara took the direct flight from Copenhagen to Nuuk, where Lars had a friend from high school. Nuuk was Greenland's capital and its largest town, with approximately 18,000 inhabitants and a sizeable ethnic Danish population. Nuuk was located on Greenland's west coast next to one of the fjords. On the opposite side of the fjord north of the town, the Sermitsiaq mountain dominated the horizon. Located just south of the Arctic Circle, the summers in Nuuk had long days with plenty of sunshine and a good deal of rainy days. Snowfall was rare at that time of the year, but the temperature could vary from around -7° to +26° Celsius.

Lars's friend Torben worked for Air Greenland and was based in Nuuk at the company's headquarters. Torben had a senior position in the company and had arranged that Lara and Lars could fly with a group of tourists and see one of the large Greenland glaciers. The summer had been unusually warm in Greenland, with record high temperatures leading to substantial melting of sea ice and glaciers. In one day in mid-summer, the melting was the equivalent of one month of melting in previous years. Torben explained that the increase in melting water from the Greenland glaciers would increase the weakening of the Gulf Stream and could lead to even more extreme weather in Europe and intensify sea-level rise at the east coast of North America.

The trip took them to the Russell Glacier on the west coast north of Nuuk. They could see the water running on the top of the glacier and the vapor in the air on top of the glacier during the hot summer day. The helicopter landed in front of the glacier, where you could hear the loud sound of the cracking ice.

Lara and her father were very close. They were both extroverts and had a passion for traveling and experiencing new places, societies, and people engaged in different fields of work. They both had curious minds and liked exploring all corners of the world. They enjoyed each other's company and, over the years, had often traveled together.

After the trip to the glacier, they had a long talk over supper in Nuuk. Lara was curious to hear Lars' assessment of the global warming crisis and his view on what could happen in the coming years and decades. Lars was an optimistic person by nature. The evolving global warming crisis and the associated effects of increasing freshwater shortages, hunger, related conflicts and refugees' situations, poverty, rapidly spreading infectious diseases, and other disasters in the world had tested his optimism regarding the collective ability to address the emerging challenges. It was as if many people, institutions, companies, politicians, and governments did not realize that the actions to avoid the worst consequences of global warming should be addressed here and now. For every year of delaying to take serious measures, the worse the effects would be for the planet and its inhabitants and the coming generations, who would pay a high price for the delayed response. Lars looked at Lara and knew that his assessment did not surprise her and that she respected his views and insights. Lara replied that she was happy to have had part of her upbringing without worrying about the planet's faith. She acknowledged that global warming and climate change would affect the rest of her life, particularly the children she was planning to have later in her life.

The sun had not yet set when they went for a late evening walk through the streets of Nuuk. People were still out on the roads, and the whole town was affected by the long days and short nights at this time of the year. Greenland had experienced warmer weather for some time, and this had already changed the rhythm and quality of life in the small capital just south of the Arctic Circle.

Chapter 7

London

Lara began her studies in London after the trip to Greenland. After a lot of thought, she had applied and was accepted to a three-year undergraduate program on Environment and Development at the London School of Economics. Lara had moved into her parents' flat on Russell Square, which was just a ten to fifteen minutes' walk from the school on Southampton Row. Lara loved London and enjoyed being close to several old friends from the International School in Geneva who now lived in and around London. Her fellow students came from all over the world, and Lara felt at home in this international and diverse environment. Her years in the international school in Geneva had prepared her well for the demanding workload involved in studying at one of the leading Universities in Great Britain. Over the years, she and her parents had visited London many times and stayed in the apartment, making her adjustment to life in London much more effortless. She was also aware that she was born in London almost twenty years ago and had often visited the area where her mother lived at the time.

The first year of her undergraduate program focused on environmental change, sustainable development, and geography, topics essential for understanding the effects in a fast-changing world. The program contained various coursework, including essays, case studies, reports, and mock exams. The students helped each other with the extensive workload and thus got to know each other very well. Lara had already made friends with a couple of the women in her class. She had been paying attention to an Indian male student from Bengaluru' Bangalore', the capital of India's southern Karnataka state. Jamal, like Lara, had had an international upbringing. His parents had been part of the rapid industrial development of Bengaluru in the 1980s and 1990s, and they had both worked in the rapidly growing tech industry in the city that became known as the Silicon Valley of India. They had joined an American company in the early 2000s and moved to the headquarter of the company in the

United States in the mid-2000s. Jamal was born in the late 2000s in Dallas, Texas, and was around five years old when the family moved to London in the mid-2010s to work for another American tech company. He and Lara were both in a group of students hanging out together at the cafes and bars around the school. They often had dinners together at either Lara's or Jamal's place. Over the first year, Lara and Jamal started seeing each other more frequently and on the weekends. Jamal was a tall, athletic person with a warm, open appearance and mind and was born with a sharp and analytical mind. They were both attracted to yoga and jogging and increasingly spent the weekends together enjoying each other's company and benefitting from the many cultural attractions in the city.

None of them would be able to say exactly when their relationship changed from a close friendship to a love relationship. Still, their fellow students had noticed it well before they had realized that they had a crush on each other. The love affair with Jamal changed Lara's life, and she began to understand what had happened when her parents had met each other in Zambia before she was born.

Great Barrier Reef

The plane touched down at Sydney International Airport. In the second year of her undergraduate program at the London School of Economics, Lara was on a field trip. She and her classmates had taken the direct roughly 17,000 kilometers flight from London to Sidney. It had taken around 20 hours, and they were pretty exhausted when they arrived in Sydney. The original plan was to continue to Cairns the same day. Still, the Northern town in Queensland had recently been hit by a category 5 cyclone that had severely damaged the town's infrastructure, including the airport. Their flight had been rescheduled to Brisbane on the east coast of Queensland, around 1,600 kilometers south of Cairns. They arrived in the afternoon and spent their first day adjusting to the time difference between London and the east coast of Australia.

The Great Barrier Reef was the world's largest and longest coral reef and stretched along the coast of Queensland for around 2,300 kilometers covering an area of approximately 344,000 square kilometers. Lara and her classmates were in the process of preparing a case study on the state of the world's coral reefs, given the increasing temperature and acidity of the seas.

Their first meeting was with a representative from the Great Barrier Reef Foundation in Brisbane. They were received by the Media Manager of the Foundation the following day. She gave them a short introduction to the Foundation and the scientific research on the Great Barrier Reef supported by the Foundation. She explained that the first damages to the reef were encountered in the late 1990s and were followed by more severe losses in the mid-2010s caused by an extended marine heatwave. Around 29 percent of the 3,863 reefs were severely damaged over nine months, and they had lost two-thirds of their corals, severely reducing their ecological functioning. It was mainly the Northern third of the reef that had been bleached and damaged during the heatwave. The corals had never fully recovered after that incident. A new, even longer marine heatwave set in a few years later, where close to 85 percent of the corals were severely damaged and had lost three-thirds of their corals, reducing their ecological footprint functioning even further. The Foundation had for many years tried to influence the politicians in Queensland and at the federal level. They had stressed that the continued global warming, use of fertilizers for farming along the coast, and coal mining in the area would eventually lead to the total degradation and bleaching of one of the seven wonders of the natural world. The Foundation feared that the continued global warming, which had already reached between 1.0°C and 1.5°C, would relatively soon lead to an irreversible loss of most of the coral reefs in the world, including the Great Barrier Reef.

In the evening, they took the train up along the east coast of Queensland towards Cairns. They reached the small town of Tully around 140 kilometers south of Cairns the next afternoon and took a bus to Mission Beach on the coast early in the evening. They stayed in one of the many beach cottages along the seashore. The purpose of the visit was to assess the socio-economic effects of the damaged reef on tourism and the environmental impact on marine life in the area. From their interviews, they learned that tourism had gone down considerably, beginning with the Cyclone Yasi in 2011, which had caused severe damage to the local infrastructure and obliterated a large resort on Dunk Island situated some five kilometers off the coast. All the corals in the area were bleached during the latest marine heatwave, and the associated tourist industry had come to a standstill.

The trip to Australia made a deep impression on Lara and her classmates. They had seen with their own eyes how one of the natural wonders of the world had been reduced to a bleached skeleton. It had a catastrophic effect on the biodiversity in the sea around the reef and the socio-economic ramifications of the loss of the otherwise pristine coral reefs along the eastern seaboard of Queensland. For many years, the Australian Government had been in denial regarding the relationship between CO_2 emission and global warming, the related warming of the oceans, and the damages to the coral reefs. Australia had for years been by far the largest exporter of coal in the world and responsible for close to 40 percent of all exports. The largest coal mines in Australia were in Queensland, not far from the Great Barrier Reef. The coal from the mines was shipped out of Australia from the Port of Hay Point, one of the largest coal export ports globally and located close to the reef.

Lara had a hard time understanding how the people in Australia had allowed the deliberate destruction of their own country by exporting vast amounts of coal, which would end up as CO_2 emissions in the atmosphere and thereby heat the country and the oceans even more. The resulting droughts and extensive wildfires that Australia had increasingly experienced and the near destruction of the Great Barrier Reef was a high price to pay for the country and the world in general.

New York

After finishing her undergraduate degree at the London School of Economics, Lara decided to move to New York and join a master's program on Global Environmental Politics at New York University. The move to New York allowed her to stay together with her grandparents in Brooklyn Heights and spend more time with them in their old age. Her grandparents were in their 80s and were frailer but still active both physically and mentally. They still had a busy social life but had stopped their work at the university some years back.

During her last years in London, Lara had increasingly focused on the transition to a green economy. She realized that the political dimension in this transition was of utmost importance. Nongovernmental organizations played a crucial role in bringing about the needed changes at the political level. Jamal and Lara had decided to break up after living together for two years in Lara's apartment in London. They realized that they needed to have the freedom to pursue different paths in their lives in the coming years and not be bound by a relationship where Lara would live in New York, and Jamal would continue with a master's degree program in London.

Lara quickly settled in New York and soon became fascinated by the many opportunities in the city and the northeastern United States, including the New England states. She was very much aware that her mother had grown up in the town and that she was following in her footsteps by living and studying in the same place. Her parents still lived in Geneva, but her father had stopped working for the World Bank and enjoyed spending his time hiking in the Jura mountains and the Alps. He had also started writing his memories from the many years of working in international development. Her mother was still doing consultancies for her company in developing countries all over the world.

Lara had many discussions with her grandparents about the world's challenges towards the end of the 2020s.

Global warming had already reached 1.5° Celsius, and the many predicted consequences of a warming planet were increasingly reflected in the weather patterns worldwide. The developing countries, especially Africa, were the worst affected, but the South Asian and Southeast Asian countries encountered growing climate change challenges and adverse effects. In the United States, many mainly low-lying areas along the Gulf Coast and Eastern Seaboard were increasingly experiencing sunny day flooding due to the rising sea level. Wildfires were becoming more severe in the western part of the United States, and droughts were more frequent and widespread. Worst of all was the increasing number of category 5 hurricanes causing widespread destruction along the Gulf Coast and Eastern Seaboard. It had become more expensive to insure property in hurricane-affected areas, and people without insurance faced increasing hardship when affected by the hurricanes. The political crisis at the end of the 2010s had delayed the response to global warming. But, during the 2020s, both the federal and state governments had accelerated the efforts to bring the United States back among the countries which took the transition to a green economy seriously.

Sahel

During the second year of the master's program at New York University, Lara's thesis project took her to the Sahel. The Sahel at the time formed a broad belt of up to 1000 kilometers stretching from the Atlantic Ocean in West Africa to the Red Sea in Northern Africa and had a semi-arid climate bordering the Southern side of the vast Sahara Desert. The Sahel region had experienced regular droughts and sometimes severe droughts that lasted more than two hundred years. The latest drought started ten years earlier and had a devastating impact in the Sahel climate zone, covering approximately 3 million square kilometers.

Before the trip to the Sahel, Sara collected all the available data and official reports on the latest drought concerning the number of internally displaced people and refugees, food shortages, water supply, health data, and the response from the countries in question and the international aid organizations. The population in the Sahel had increased rapidly in the previous decades and had passed 200 million people. Given the semi-arid climate and the increasingly unstable weather in the region, it had already been challenging to secure food and drinking water for the population in the area before the latest drought period. The drought had forced millions of people to migrate to places with access to shelter, food, and drinking water. Countries in the region had established numerous camps for internally displaced people and refugees from the countries in the region with assistance from the international community. The international aid agencies had had severe problems raising the financial resources to cater to the people in the refugee camps, given the ongoing climate-related disasters hitting countries worldwide with a frequency and intensity never seen before in modern times. Nobody knew when the drought would stop, and there was increasing tension between the people who had migrated to the camps and the people already living in the areas around the camps. Some of the countries in the region had already experienced conflicts before the drought, which had escalated to civil wars in some countries. Heatwaves with temperatures up to 44 °C were recorded more frequently in the Sahel, making outdoor life close to impossible.

The visit to the refugee camp just outside the Northern outskirts of Ouagadougou was the most disturbing experience during Lara's three months of travel to study the effect of the ongoing drought in the Sahel region. One of the largest, the camp housed around half a million internally displaced people from Burkina Faso and refugees from primarily Mali and Niger.

With Lara's privileged background, it was hard to comprehend people's conditions in the camp, the insecurity they had endured in the areas they came from, and the risks associated with traveling for many days and weeks through the Sahel. Confronted with the situation in the Sahel, Lara increasingly felt that the world leaders were doing too little too late to address the escalating disasters.

Labor Day Revisited

The Labor Day Hurricane in 1935 was the most intense Atlantic hurricane to make landfall on record and tied with Hurricane Dorian in 2019 as the strongest landfalling Atlantic hurricane by maximum sustained winds of 185 miles per hour. The Labor Day hurricane was one of four category 5 hurricanes on record to strike the USA mainland. Several islands in the Florida Keys had nearly all their structures destroyed, and close to 250 people lost their life.

It was the end of a long hot, and humid summer in Miami a century later. Over the past twenty years, the area around Miami had seen an increasing number of sunny day floods with rising seawater in low-lying areas associated with events such as full and new moons. These tidal floods had led to substantial investments in raising roads and improvements to the sewer systems in low-lying areas and the installation of pump systems to reduce the degree of the flooding.

It had been an unusually calm year with few tropical storms and no hurricanes making landfall in Florida. A tropical depression had formed in the Atlantic at the end of August and had gradually moved up East of the Lesser Antilles. As it intensified, it was named Sheba and had formed an eye the same day. It was a slow-moving system growing in size and strength as it moved north of the Greater Antilles in early September. Sheba had developed into a category 3 hurricane off the North coast of Puerto Rico. At that stage, The National Hurricane Center issued a warning that it might develop into a category 5 hurricane before making landfall on the East coast of Florida. At that time, the Governor of Florida had issued a mandatory evacuation order for the roughly 10 million people living along the state's Atlantic coast. Sheba gained strength as it moved north of Cuba and became a category 5 hurricane as it approached the Florida East coast on Labor Day with wind speeds of up to 185 miles per hour. It made landfall on Miami Beach close to midnight the same day with a storm tide of close to thirty feet.

The hurricane's strong winds and surge destroyed nearly all non-concrete structures on Miami Beach, which was submerged under the storm surge. Cars, yachts, and debris were floating in between the concrete apartment blocks and hotels. The few remaining inhabitants were standing on the rooftops waving to the many rescue helicopters in the early morning hours after the hurricane had passed the metropolitan area, which had around six million people before the hurricane. The many pumps installed to reduce the flooding on the mainland to protect the low-lying areas were overwhelmed by the storm surge, and large parts of Miami City were flooded and without electricity and water supply. With close to 1,500 deaths in the USA, Hurricane Sheba was the deadliest hurricane to hit the mainland in the 21st Century. Close to a million people lost their homes, and damages to the tune of USD 500 billion made Sheba the costliest hurricane on record.

The hurricane was a wake-up call for the population in Southern Florida. It was clear that the metropolitan area of Miami and the Southern part of the state would never be rebuilt, and assessments were made to determine which part of the state to inhabit in the future decades. In the immediate aftermath of the hurricane, prices on the property started to fall, leaving many people without savings and mortgages higher than the value of the properties. It had been expected that Southern Florida could be sustained up to around the 2050s-2060s, but Hurricane Sheba had pushed the timeline 10-20 years in the wrong direction. A smaller version of Miami emerged over the years that incorporated platform houses and floating structures. Still, the City of Miami was no longer a vibrant city with many million inhabitants.

Veronica

Lara joined a Ph.D. program at New York University in Public Administration after finishing her master's degree. She had chosen the program because she was interested in conducting research related to environmental policies and sustainable development. She also managed to combine the Ph.D. program with an internship at the Unicef Headquarters in New York during the first year of her program.

Her grandparents had moved to the west coast of Costa Rica to benefit from the warmth, sun, and rich nature just north of the Equator. Lara's parents had taken over the flat in Brooklyn Heights and refurbished it so that Lara could use it during the coming years in New York. Lara was still relatively young and saw herself as a world citizen, with friends living in many countries. Most of her friends were from her time in the International School in Geneva, and almost all of them were still busy with their education. During her vacations, Lara traveled with her friends or visited them where they were doing their studies. Many were based in or in the vicinity of London, which allowed Lara to visit London and use her parents' flat in the center of the city. She was very much aware of her privileged life. She realized that she would use her professional skills to make a difference for people, especially in developing countries, who were less privileged and could not get many of their most basic needs in life met.

It was becoming more and more evident that the world leaders and countries were failing to live up to the green transition and the sustainable development goals. Much time and energy had been wasted on trade wars, regional conflicts, and domestic issues. Most people in the world had still not realized the devastating consequences of inaction related to the increasing climate changes in the world. More and more resources were spent mitigating the damages and preventing further destructions to especially cities in coastal areas, and not enough on reducing CO_2 emissions to levels that would be compatible with the survival of our civilization.

Lara benefited in many ways from her internship at Unicef's Division of Communication which kept her informed about the global trends in children's health, nutritional status, and wellbeing. It was clear from the data that children in drought and flooding affected areas had seen an increasing deterioration in their health and nutritional status over the last decades. On the positive side, it was clear that the introduction of modern vaccines in most countries had continued to benefit children's health and nutritional status and significantly reduced child mortality, especially in developing countries. She had already decided that her research under her Ph.D. program would focus on the relationship between climate change and child health in developing countries. She would use child mortality rates as the most important indicator for assessing trends in children's health.

Lara also enjoyed meeting the many different employees from all over the world and hearing about their experiences and upbringing. She often went for lunch with colleagues in the United Nations headquarter cafeteria on the ground floor in the Secretariat Building overlooking the East River. Lara was mainly hanging out with the many Junior Professional Officers but would occasionally have lunch with senior staff members. She had met Veronica at one of the many seminars on child health in Unicef. She had been impressed with her presentation on the importance of health education and communication in developing countries. They had talked a couple of times during the lunch break, and Veronica had taken a keen interest in Lara's Ph. D. research on climate change and child health. Veronica had joined Unicef in New York after working for several years in Africa for the British Government's development agency. She had first trained as a nurse-midwife in England and later took a master's degree in health education and promotion at the University of Edinburgh.

They both lived in Brooklyn and had started jogging together during the weekends along Brooklyn Heights and across the Brooklyn Bridge to Manhattan. They had enjoyed each other's company from the first time they met, and over the months, they had taken a keen interest in each other's lives. Lara had always had close female and male friends and had always been fascinated by women who were a bit older than her. She studied how they dressed, their attitude towards other people, and how they communicated their viewpoints, feelings, and perspectives on life in general. Since her time in London, Lara had not had a long-term relationship and was missing the love and intimacy such a relationship could bring into one's life. What was new for Lara this time was to be attracted to another woman in this way. Lara knew that Veronica had had previous relationships with men but was unaware of any relationships with women. Lara was aware that something was happening in her friendship with Veronica and noticed any hints that pointed to Veronica being attracted to her.

Florence

It had been an unusually wet and hot spring in Florence that year. The tourists were still coming to the city in Tuscany in great numbers to visit what had been the center of medieval European trade and finance and one of the wealthiest cities of that era. By the beginning of June, the weather in Florence had become exceptionally hot and humid.

Déborah, a medical doctor specializing in pediatrics, was on call at the university hospital in Florence during one of the first weekends in June. On a Saturday, Déborah had admitted a 5-year-old boy to the hospital with fever, vomiting, joint pain, and headache. She was surprised to see a child with these symptoms at this time of the year but had admitted the boy for observation to rule out a potential severe infectious disease. On Sunday, she had to admit two more children with the same symptoms from the same low-lying area of the city. The boy had now developed a slight rash on his chest and was not getting better. Déborah, who had worked in the United States after finishing her medical degree in Italy, was beginning to suspect that this cluster of children with similar symptoms could point to an outbreak of an infectious disease in the city. The lab tests on the boy indicated that he was suffering from a viral infection and that the infection had suppressed the number of platelets in his blood. None of the children had traveled outside Italy during the last months, which ruled out malaria or other tropical diseases.

At the pediatric department meeting Monday morning, it was decided that since all three children attended the same school, they should all have a spinal tap to collect cerebrospinal fluid to exclude the possibility of a meningitis epidemic in the area. Later the same day, another three children were admitted to the hospital with the same symptoms. The tests on the cerebrospinal fluid from the three first children were negative, which led the department's head to contact the Centre for Tropical Diseases in Verona for assistance to rule out a potential outbreak of a tropical disease in Florence. They advised the pediatric department to test the children for Dengue fever, Zika, and Chikungunya. These three viral diseases were all transmitted by the Aedes mosquitoes, which were widespread in Northern, Central, and Southern Italy and responsible for the previous outbreaks of Chikungunya in Italy during the last twenty years.

Only one of the children tested positive for Dengue Fever, but it was well-known that the test could be negative in the first days of the infection. In the following weeks, a total of 38 people, including more than twenty children, were identified as being infected with the Dengue virus from the same area in the city. It was the first major outbreak of Dengue in Italy and Europe, which until this outbreak only had seen sporadic cases of local transmission of the Dengue virus in Spain and France.

It meant that the whole of the Mediterranean area was now at risk for an increasing number of epidemics of Dengue Fever, Zika, and Chikungunya. They were all related to global warming and frequent travels to tropical areas where the three diseases had spread to almost all corners of the world.

Costa Rica

Lara's life took a new turn with the news of her grandfather's death in Costa Rica. He had suffered a heart attack one morning while swimming in the Pacific Ocean and was found drowned on the beach not far from his home. Lara had been very attached to her grandfather, and his death was her first experience with losing a loved one. Lara's grandmother had decided that her grandfather should be honored in a ceremony on the beach where he had died, and his ashes spread out on the ocean after the ceremony. Lara met her parents in Miami before flying down to the west coast of Costa Rica. Her grandparents' cottage was in Playa Hermosa, less than a half-hour drive from the airport. Her parents had booked rooms for them in the Hotel El Velero in the center of the town, close to the beachfront. Lara was in her mid-twenties at the time and at an age where death and dying seemed very strange and beyond comprehension. She was aware that her parents were getting older but saw them as part of the very foundation of her life and refused to accept the fact that they would not always be there.

The ceremony took place the following day with old friends from her grandparents' time at the university, local friends from the town, and people who had helped them settle in when they moved to Costa Rica. It was a bright sunny morning, and the hotel had helped her grandmother arrange the ceremony. Standing together with her daughter, she gave a speech in honor of her grandfather and the long adventurous life they had lived together. One by one, their close friends stood up and reflected on their long friendship with their grandparents. It was a very moving ceremony which was concluded when a boat transported the urn out to the sea and spread her grandfather's ashes on the water around the boat. They then all gathered in the courtyard of the hotel for a reception in honor of her grandfather.

Lara left Costa Rica a few days later. Her parents stayed behind to help her grandmother with all the administrative issues related to her grandfather's death. Her grandmother had decided to live with her parents in Geneva after her husband's death which meant that Lara's parents had to help her pack all her things for the move to Switzerland and arrange for a caretaker of the cottage in Playa Hermosa. Her parents had decided to retain the ownership of the cottage. Lara was more touched by the death of her grandfather than she had expected. He was an older man and had lived a full life, and death had come to him while he was still active and engaged in his and his family's lives. Her grandfather had often mentioned that it would not be a misfortune if he died at his age and that he felt fortunate and grateful for having lived a privileged life. He had seen his daughter grow up to become a warm and successful person, and he had spent time with his only grandchild. He saw life as a gift and had often indicated that he hoped that all his family members would pursue a deep and rewarding life and remember all the good times they had had together even after his death. Lara had never experienced an actual loss in her life, and over the last week, she had increasingly felt the grief and sorrow of losing her grandfather and realizing that he would never be there in her life again.

The journey on the plane back to New York gave her time to reflect on her life and her emotions in connection with her grandfather's death. Veronica kept on popping up in her mind, and she was increasingly becoming aware of the fact that she meant more to her than she had been willing to admit previously. She landed in Newark and took the train to the apartment in Brooklyn Heights. The apartment came across as being empty and lifeless after the intense days in Playa Hermosa. After unpacking her suitcase, she went down to the local supermarket on Montague Street to fill up her empty refrigerator. Lara was a vegetarian but loved yogurt and cheese, knowing it was recommended to cut down on dairy products to save the planet. She called Veronica on the way back to the apartment and hoped she was in town and had no plans for the evening. She was relieved to hear Veronica's calm voice filled with empathy and warmth.

Lara quickly prepared a vegetable lasagna for the evening meal with Veronica and had purchased a lot of fruit for a dessert and a bottle of chianti for the lasagna. Veronica arrived later in the evening and hugged Lara as she entered the apartment. Lara could no longer hold back her tears and, for the first time, allowed herself to feel the deep pain associated with the death of her grandfather. Veronica held Lara close to her in a warm embrace and allowed her to cry without saying a word. They were both aware that they were letting their feelings for each other come out in a full display. Lara lifted her head from Veronica's shoulder, looked her in the eyes, and smiled with tears running down her cheeks. They kissed each other for a long time and made love in Lara's bedroom. They were both surprised with how quickly their friendship had turned into a sexual relationship, and they spent the rest of the evening trying to understand what had happened between them.

The relationship with Veronica was a turning point in Lara's life. She felt that their relationship and deep understanding and caring for each other gave her life new meaning and an inner purpose. She also thought that she had much more energy and inspiration in her day-to-day life and work. Her internship at Unicef was coming to an end, and she was spending more and more of her time on the thesis for her Ph.D. program at New York University. Her head of department in Unicef was interested in her research and had arranged that Lara could continue to have access to Unicef's data after the end of her internship.

Lara visited her parents and grandmother in Geneva with Veronica that summer and took Veronica to the many places around Geneva that she had enjoyed during her childhood. She also had an opportunity to introduce Veronica to some of her childhood friends visiting Geneva at the time. Some of her friends still had parents living in the

Geneva area. Lara and Veronica spent the days hiking in the Jura Mountains and the Alps, taking boat trips on Lake Geneva, or going to one of the many beaches on the Northern side of the lake. Carole had stopped working after her father's death and spent her time with her mother in the Geneva area. Lars had stopped working some years back but was still doing the odd consulting job for the World Bank. Their house on the Northern shore of Lake Geneva was overlooking the lake with the Alps, including Mont Blanc on the horizon. Lara and Veronica had most of their dinners on the terrace in front of the house, and they were often responsible for preparing the meals. Some evenings, they would visit one of the many restaurants on either the Swiss or the French side of the border. The two of them had developed a close and trusting relationship over the past months and enjoyed each other's company, and increasingly shared their life whenever they had the opportunity to spend time together. Veronica traveled extensively in her work at Unicef, and Lara had to devote a substantial amount of her free time to her research with her Ph.D. program.

Lara concluded her internship at Unicef after the summer vacation in Geneva. She initiated the fieldwork for her thesis, which involved many trips to countries worldwide to obtain more detailed data on the factors that affected children's health in the evolving climate crisis. It was becoming increasingly clear that children, especially in drought and flooding-affected areas of the world, were paying an exceedingly high price for the accelerating effects of global warming. The nutritional status of the children in the affected regions was rapidly deteriorating, and the international organizations were increasingly unable to respond to the demands of the affected children. Given the increase in natural disasters around the globe, it was getting harder and harder for the agencies to raise the funding for relief efforts in developing countries. It was as if the world's rich countries were focusing more on their own needs and were turning a blind eye to the suffering of millions of people in acute need of assistance in many low- and middle-income countries.

World Health Organization

Lara moved to Geneva two years after finishing her Ph.D. in New York. She had managed to get a job with Unicef in New York related to the topics she had addressed in her thesis. She had joined the department in the organization, which was focused on reorienting the whole organization to better respond to climate emergencies all over the world. Two years into her new job in Unicef, Lara had applied for a Junior Professional Officer position with the World Health Organization. She had been called for an interview a few months after submitting her application. The Junior Professional Officer Program gave young graduates pursuing a career in international development a structured learning experience and exposure to practical experience in international development work. Lara benefitted from the fact that she had dual citizenship and had been sponsored by the Danish Government for the position in Geneva.

She was assigned to WHO's Immunization Program at the organization's headquarter and worked with developing new strategies to ensure that the increasing number of displaced populations would be immunized with modern, effective vaccines against the leading infectious diseases in the world. A Norwegian Medical Doctor in his mid-40's headed the Immunization Department. He had a solid working experience for Unicef in Africa and had previously worked for the Norwegian Government's development agency. Jakob was a modern manager and gave a lot of responsibility to the individual members of the immunization team. Given Lara's Danish background, she could communicate with him in Danish if necessary.

Lara had found a relatively inexpensive flat for rent in the Grand-Saconnex area of the city, which was within walking distance from WHO's, Unicef's, and the Global Vaccine Alliance's respective headquarters in Geneva. She spent some of her weekends with her parents and her grandmother not far from the city center on the Northern side of Lake Geneva, close to the Jura mountains. Her grandmother was now old and frail, and Lara knew that she would probably not live much longer. Her grandmother focused all her energy on Lara when she visited and was always keen to hear about her life and experience as a young woman in her late 20's. Lara's parents were also getting older but were still active and in good health. They were engaged in nongovernmental and voluntary work with a strong focus on sustainable development and the transition to a green economy.

Jakob quickly realized that Lara was an asset to the department with her extensive experience working with Unicef and excellent English and French language skills. Lara had a positive and energetic approach to her work and loved working in small groups with people from all over the world. She traveled extensively with Jakob during the first year of her assignment. They developed a close relationship and enjoyed each other's company. Jakob was single but had a large family in Norway and many close friends in Geneva. He loved the outdoor life and spent the weekends hiking, bicycling, or skiing in the mountains around Lake Geneva. He was very fit, funny, and hardworking, and Lara learned a lot from him concerning health development and immunization programs.

On a trip with Jakob to a refugee camp in the Horn of Africa, Lara was called by her mother and informed about her grandmother's death. Lara knew that her grandmother was not well, but her death came as a shock to her. Her grandmother had been a warm, loving person throughout her life and a person she could talk to about all aspects of her life. She was caring and a good listener with a lot of life experience and wisdom. Lara was far away from the nearest airport, and it would take some days before she could join her parents in Geneva. Jakob was very understanding and quickly arranged that Lara could be driven to the international airport in Addis Ababa in Ethiopia. She spent the evening with Jakob in his tent, had dinner, and talked about life and death and their experience with losing loved ones. Lara told Jakob about her grandparents and the death of her grandfather some years back in Costa Rica. Jakob still had his parents, but all his grandparents had died earlier in his life. Like Lara, he had not been in Norway at their death and was aware of the challenges and emotions of being away from one's family when a close relative passed away. Lara cried on and off throughout the evening but felt safe and comforted in Jakob's company. They were both aware that they liked each other, but Lara had never seen Jakob as a potential lover. However, there was something special going on between them that evening when Lara's emotions were raw and volatile, and she was more sensitive to Jakob's warm and open personality. They had occasionally hugged and kissed each other in a purely friendly way, but towards the end of the evening, as Lara was on her way out of the tent, she gave Jakob a warm embrace and could feel how her emotions towards him rushed through her whole body. They stood and looked at each other for a short while to sense what was happening between them. Lara put her head on his shoulder and started to cry again, but at the same time, she could feel how her body was ready to make love with Jakob. Half crying and half-smiling, she dragged him to his bed in the corner of the tent and began to undress in front of him. He quickly undressed, pulled her close to him under the bed cover, and they made love in the quiet, cold desert night.

They woke up in each other's arms early the next morning and smiled at each other, both surprised by how their relationship had suddenly turned into a love affair. They were aware that they had to be careful since Jakob was her boss, and they were in a relatively small working environment at WHO.

That morning, Lara was picked up from the camp by a Unicef vehicle and drove throughout the day before reaching Addis Ababa airport late in the evening. She was lucky to get a direct flight to Frankfurt the same evening. Later that night, she was sitting by herself, looking out into the dark African night some 40,000 feet above the Sahara Dessert. Her head was full of thoughts and conflicting emotions. She was sad and joyful at the same time and could still feel the embrace by Jakob's warm body the previous night. She had not made love to a man for many years and had not made love to anyone since she left New York. She was aware that she was both attracted to women and men but had for some time found herself being more attracted to women.

Carole picked her up at the airport in Geneva and took Lara to the family house close to Nyon on the Northern side of Lake Geneva. It was a bright, sunny autumn day with a clear view of Mont Blanc from her parent's house. After a short shower, Lara went for a walk with her mother in the foothills of the Jura mountains, a short distance from the home. Carole had known for some time that her mother's health was deteriorating and that it was just a matter of time before she would die. Lara and Carole walked arm in arm along the small paths in the woods on the mountain slopes. They talked about the many journeys they had had together with her mother and their lives in New York and Geneva. Lara was conscious that she could not understand what losing her father or her mother would mean. They had been there throughout her life and were in many ways the foundation of her life and were always there if she needed their help or wanted to share an experience or challenge in her life. They had created a family circle of love, respect, and trust where she felt that they shared their respective lives in an open and attentive atmosphere. She had never had conflicts with her parents, and even in her teenage years, her parents understood that her mood swings had nothing to do with them but were related to her challenges in growing up as a young woman.

Lara's grandmother had insisted that they should not arrange a formal funeral for her but had wanted that the three of them should spread her ashes on Lake Geneva after her death. Lara spent the rest of the week with her parents, and they had many moments where they talked about Carole's parents and their long life in New York, Florida, Virgin Islands, and Costa Rica and her grandmother's final years in Geneva. Lara shared her recent love affair with Jakob with her parents and mentioned that she had begun thinking about having a child before getting too old in the past year. She also said that the idea of giving birth to a child was not without having second thoughts regarding what was going on in the world concerning the severe climate crisis, which was getting more acute every year. What kind of life would a child have in such a world, and would there even be a semblance of civilization to make a meaningful life on Earth possible by the end of the Century?

Chapter 16

Meaning in Life

Lara had just turned thirty when she finished her assignment with the WHO in Geneva. During the past two years, she had traveled worldwide and had seen the impact that global warming had on people's lives and livelihood. The low- and middle-income countries were the worst affected, and the number of people living in temporary refugee camps increased by millions every year. The competition for scarce resources led to an increasing number of conflicts between and within countries and a growing prevalence of failed states.

Lara knew that she had been very privileged but was increasingly aware that her life as a global citizen, having lived on three continents, also had its challenges. After turning 30, she began asking herself several existential questions. Who am I? Where am I? Where am I going? were some of the questions she felt she had to confront in her life. She had enjoyed the relationship with Jacob over the last year. Still, she was not ready to commit to a more formal relationship when he was offered a senior position in New York with Unicef. She knew that she wanted to have children at a given point, but she was still not ready to dedicate her life to a man and the prospect of having children at this stage in her life. The obvious career path would be to follow in her father's footsteps and pursue a career in international development. But given the challenges in the world, how could such a career contribute to addressing them when the consequences of global warming were bringing the world closer and closer to an untenable scenario.

She had become increasingly aware of the need for people to take an active stand against the forces driving global warming, be it in the energy, transport, or agricultural sectors. It was not enough to leave it to the politicians at the national, regional, or worldwide level to guide the world in the right direction. The Sustainable Development Goals had not been reached in 2030. Many countries were way behind in fulfilling their national goals in reducing CO_2 emissions and preventing the ongoing warming of the planet. The global temperature had already risen to 2 degrees Celsius above pre-industrial levels, with all the predicted consequences playing out every month in the form of heatwaves, droughts, wildfires, severe storms, floods, increased number of epidemics, reduced food production, and rapid extinction of flora and fauna. Time was running out for the civilization as it had been known. For Lara, it was a moment to reflect on the meaning of her life in the context of the relatively few years left before the fabric of the society would be coming apart.

Lara had heard that a Danish grass-roots organization was looking for people with an international background and with language skills to assist them in their work related to the green agenda and the mobilization of people and organizations all over Europe and the world at large. The World in Our Hands grass-root movement was part of the United Nations Agenda to raise awareness and action related to climate change. Within a few weeks, Lara was heading to Copenhagen to start a new chapter in her life as a member of the team leading the Danish organization, which had its headquarters in Copenhagen. She was extremely excited about living in Denmark for the first time in her life and having more time to spend with her older siblings, who were still based in Copenhagen. She had deliberately booked her flight to Copenhagen on one of the planes fueled with hydrogen recently introduced by the major airlines in Europe. All planes had for some time been mandated to use biofuel within Europe, but the airline industry's future was based on converting to hydrogen-powered planes.

Denmark had been at the forefront of the green agenda, and Lara was aware that one of the largest hydrogen production facilities in the world was based close to the airport in Copenhagen. On the approach to the airport, the plane took a turn around the seaway separating Denmark and Sweden, and she was able to see the many sea-based wind farms in the area. Denmark's power production had been based solely on renewable energy for many years. The surplus from the massive wind farms surrounding the country was either exported to the neighboring countries or used to produce hydrogen for powering planes, ships, trucks, or buses. Diesel-powered vehicles had been banned from entering the capital for some time. The national road pricing system ensured that the vehicles using the national road system paid for the construction and maintenance of the system.

Lara had found an apartment on the seafront close to Copenhagen airport. The apartment was also not far from the city center. It was situated in one of the newer parts of the city with good public transport infrastructure, plenty of bicycle lanes, and recreational areas with beaches and parks along the coastline. The Danish office of The World in Our Hands was based in an old factory converted to a community center for grassroots organizations by the Copenhagen municipality. It was only a 15-minute bicycle ride from Lara's new apartment.

Chapter 17

The World in Our Hands

Lara's new workplace was at the forefront of a global movement that aimed at mobilizing ordinary people to be part of a movement to save civilization before it was too late. It was realized at the time that only a broad popular understanding and support would allow societies to commit to the changes needed in the transition from a fossil fuel-based society to a green low CO_2 emission society. It also required a significant shift in people's diets, with reduced lamb, pork, and beef consumption. Like many others, the organization was funded through crowdfunding supplemented by various foundations and government grants. It was linked to an international network of grass-root organizations that had gained momentum after it became clear that the national and international efforts to reduce global warming had failed.

The Danish branch had a core staff of four full-time staff assisted by a large group of young volunteers and some experienced senior members who had dedicated their time to help the organization in its work. A political scientist headed the organization with solid experience in media and communication. Two staff members were engaged full-time with the website and social media, and the last team member was responsible for raising funds, financing, and accounts. They were all in their thirties and had thus been born into an inherently unsustainable society that was rapidly moving towards the abyss. Lara primarily liaised with national and international organizations and represented the Danish branch in international meetings and teleconferences.

The focus of the website and social media content was to inform people about the trend and consequences of global warming and actions people could take to influence the politicians and leaders in their workplaces, as well as concrete things people could do themselves to minimize their CO_2 footprint and to mobilize support for the organization. There were smaller branches throughout the country, which mobilized people in their area and influenced local politicians to allocate more resources for the green transition.

Lara felt at home in the organization and enjoyed the work with the staff and the many volunteers. From her many visits and holidays in Denmark, she knew that the Danes were easygoing and had a well-developed ability to function in social groups. Still, it was her first experience working in such a setting. Denmark had a long tradition of being an egalitarian society where the salary gap between high- and low-income people was one of the lowest in the world. That, combined with a well-functioning educational, health, and social security system, made the society safe, creative, and productive. She dedicated all her time to the work, and it took some time before she had time to explore the city and the country.

Given the nature of her work, she spent a lot of time working together with Frederik, who was heading the organization. He was easy-going and very supportive of her work, and they quickly realized that they shared many common interests concerning society, films, yoga, and fitness. He was tall, blond, and mild-mannered He had an air of calmness and warmth in his behavior, which made people feel at ease in his presence. Lara knew that she had been attracted to him from their first encounter but kept telling herself that she should not get involved in a new relationship this quickly. Frederik was single at the time but had recently left a long-term relationship with a Danish woman.

Lara spent many weekends with her Danish sister, Katja, and her brother, Kasper. They were both in their late thirties and had married and had two kids each, which seemed to be the Danish standard at the time. She had always enjoyed being with her siblings, which allowed her to hear more about her father when he lived in Denmark with his former wife. Lara had occasionally met Helle at weddings and other important family events. She had recently celebrated her seventieth birthday, had retired, and enjoyed spending several days every week with her grandchildren. Lara had always had a good relationship with Helle and was impressed with how she had handled the divorce from her father and established a loving and caring home for her two siblings with Aaron, whom she had married after the divorce. Helle and her mother Carole had quite different personalities, and Lara often wondered what made her father leave his Danish family when he met her mother. They were both successful in their working life, intelligent, sporty, and good-looking. Carole tended to be more easy-going, but they were both very attentive and good communicators. The two different cultures certainly made a difference. Still, Lara quite liked the Danish 'hygge' mentality and the fact that the Danes

had managed to create an egalitarian society that benefitted most
of the people in the country.

Chapter 18

Civilization

Modern civilization in the 21st Century could be visualized as a layer cake. Each layer played a vital function in society: health, education, banking, communication, transport, energy, industry, agriculture, and trade. All the layers were interconnected and had developed into increasingly more complex entities that were vulnerable to rapid changes in societies and the environment. Most people in rich countries took the functions of modern societies for granted and expected that they would continue in the foreseeable future. There would be clean potable water in the taps; buses, trains, and planes would be available when needed and operate on schedule; food would be available in stores, restaurants, and fast-food outlets; and it would be possible to pay for services all over the world using the smartphone. For most people in low- and middle-income countries, however, that had never been the case.

During the 21st century, several wake-up calls had reminded people in high-income countries that the backbone of modern society could not be taken for granted. The two latest Coronavirus pandemics had shown that the functions of contemporary society could be challenged by such events and at the same time exposed how ill-prepared modern civilization was to handle a crisis of such a nature. In both cases, effective vaccines had been developed within a year, but when it came to the challenges related to global warming, vaccines would not solve the problems. And instead of having pandemics once in ten or twenty years, the global warming catastrophes were now coming every year in the form of heatwaves, droughts, wildfires, floods, severe storms, and refugee emergencies exposing the vulnerabilities in modern civilization.

All these combined influenced modern societies where the birthrate had been going down rapidly within the last decades at the same time as populations were aging all over the world. Close to a third of the population in the high-income countries was now above 65 years of age, putting an enormous strain on the social welfare and health systems and undermining the pension systems' ability to sustain elderly citizens' livelihood.

Due to the ill-informed immigration policies of high-income countries, there was an acute lack of warm hands to provide the services needed for the aging population and a shortage of taxpayers to sustain the increasing cost of the welfare systems. Most politicians had abdicated their responsibility of informing their constituencies of the challenges facing the respective countries, thereby delaying the needed reforms to address the increasing challenges in society. The pillars of modern societies were increasingly undermined. Many citizens were increasingly looking for an easy solution to society's many problems and turning to populist movements promising to solve the challenges.

Social scientists, political observers, and journalists were fiercely debating how long the modern civilization would last and were increasingly of the opinion that it was a matter of decades at best.

Chapter 19

Where Are We Going?

Lara enjoyed her work in Copenhagen. After a couple of years, she felt that she had settled in Denmark and was part of an extensive network of people, including a group of close friends related to her organization's work. Lara and Frederik had shared many work functions and had traveled together extensively to international and domestic meetings. They enjoyed each other's company, and over the last years, they increasingly shared bits and pieces of their lives and significant aspects of their beliefs and moral and ethical standpoints.

Lara believed she had been able to suppress her feelings for Frederik and maintained that she should not become involved in a serious relationship for the time being. That all changed when she realized that Frederik was having an affair with one of the young volunteers in the organization. One thing was to suppress her true feelings for Frederik when he was single. It became much more complicated when she was confronted with a situation where Frederik was emotionally involved with another woman at their working place. She had at first convinced herself that it was not her role to judge Frederik's relationship with another woman. Lara was increasingly aware of the fact that Frederik meant more to her than she had allowed herself to admit. She also realized that she did not know Frederik's feelings towards her and if he saw her as a potential partner.

Her extensive workload and her close relationship with her family and a few female friends helped her deal with the conflicting feelings towards Frederik. She still worked a lot with Frederik and hoped that he did not sense that their relationship had changed after he had started dating another colleague. That all changed when she had news from Switzerland that her father, Lars, had had a skiing accident and was in a coma at a local hospital. Lars was in his early seventies, but he had been in good health and a very active hiker and skier until the accident. During a meeting with Frederik the same afternoon to discuss her travel plans and pending work, she had trouble controlling her emotions towards her father and Frederik. Lars had been a very central and close, caring person throughout her life, and Lara could not envision a life without him. He was always there when she needed him for advice, love, tenderness, and care. They had traveled together extensively worldwide, and she had never been in doubt of his love and support. Frederik and Lars had much in common, and being confronted with Frederik in the meeting and her raw emotions concerning her father were too much for her. She could not help crying during the meeting with Frederik and express how worried she was about her father's condition. Frederik listened to her with his usual warm demeanor and allowed her to cry without asking many questions. He just went over and gave her a warm embrace. At that moment, they both realized that their feelings for each other were more profound than a friendship.

Lara was on the late evening flight to Geneva the same day and had had many phone calls with her mother throughout the day. Lars had been hit by another skier and had hurt his head when falling. The ski helmet had most likely saved his life. He had been conscious in the helicopter on the way to the hospital but had slipped into a coma later in the afternoon. The scan had revealed intracranial bleeding, and the last thing Lara had heard was that he was undergoing surgery at the University Hospital.

She was met by her mother, Carole, at the airport, and they went straight to the hospital to get the latest news about

Lars' condition. He was still in a coma after the surgery, but they were allowed to sit by his bed at the intensive care unit. It was a long night for both, with a thousand feelings and events passing through their minds. In many respects, they had shared their whole life with Lars, and for both of them, he was a key figure in their lives. The early light from the rising sun shone on Mont Blanc when Lars started showing signs of coming out of the coma. He was very confused but could feel their presence on both sides of his bed. It took some time before he understood what had happened to him, and he had no recollection of the accident or the helicopter trip to the hospital.

Lara stayed with Carole in Geneva over the weekend. By Monday, it was clear that Lars would survive the accident but that it might take many weeks and potentially months for him to recover from the head injury he had sustained. Lara had had close contact with her siblings throughout the weekend and had also given Helle a call to let her know about Lars' accident. Lara went back to Copenhagen on the Tuesday morning flight in time to catch up on her work. During her stay, she had told her mother about the position she had applied for in the Danish Foreign Service. She had already attended one interview at the ministry in Copenhagen.

She met with Frederik the following day. They had an open office setting, but Frederik had suggested using one of the small meeting rooms for the meeting. He began the meeting by saying that he knew that they were in a working place with few full-time workers. It was important for everyone to know that such a setting required a very open dialogue on important issues affecting all employees. He smiled and acknowledged that it was a very formal way of starting a meeting and asked Lara about her father's health situation. Lara explained that Lars had been discharged from the hospital and was resting at home but still did not know how the accident would affect his cognitive skills in the medium to long term. Lara smiled and thanked Frederik for his support the previous week. Frederik smiled back and tried to concentrate on what he had planned to share with Lara. Frederik was aware that what he was about to say had been on his mind since last week. Frederik mentioned that he had had very few long-term relationships with women in his life and that from the moment he and Lara had met, he had realized that they had many interests, views, and beliefs in common. He had been attracted to her from the first day she entered the office. He mentioned that he had just ended a long-term relationship with a woman and had decided to take some time to understand the reasons for their mutual agreement to end the relationship. He mentioned that he had sensed last week that something was going on between them at a deeper emotional level and wanted to understand better if Lara had had a similar emotional experience. Lara was now trying hard to understand all the emotions running through her mind at the same time. She looked at Frederik with tears running down her cheeks and went over to him, sat on his lap, gave him a big hug, and kissed him on his lips. She felt a deep sense of warmth and relief in her whole body and had a feeling of wanting to be close to him in a more intimate way. Frederik was for once short of words. He just looked at her smiling, open face and used his hand to remove some of the tears from her cheeks. After some time, Lara asked him, 'What happens next?' Frederik had had time to reflect on what was going on between them and suggested that Lara join him for dinner in his apartment the same evening.

Frederik had a flat in the central part of the city overlooking one of the three lakes that gave the city a recreational area at its very center. The place had over time been covered with a growing number of bars, cafés, and restaurants. In the summer, the whole area turned into a bustling scene with crowds of mainly young people enjoying the lakes during the day and filling the bars, cafés, and restaurants in the evening and into the night. Lara had changed her clothing three times before leaving her flat and was still doubtful if she had chosen the right outfit on her way to Frederik's flat. It was still early spring where the days could be cold in this part of Europe, so she had taken the Metro. Her mind had been quite chaotic the whole day since the morning encounter with Frederik, and Lara was still surprised that she had reacted so emotionally and directly to the situation. Was she ready to have an intimate relationship with him, and what would that mean in the context of their working relationship at the office? The train came to a stop at the Metro station close to Frederik's flat. She took the stairs up to the street level to warm her body and clear her mind. It was only a five-minute walk to his flat. She deliberately pushed all her previous thoughts out of her mind and concentrated on navigating the traffic and the many people walking around in the area. When she arrived at his flat, she noticed that she had never really paid attention to Frederik's surname and noticed that there was only one name related to his flat. She had deliberately not asked Frederik about his recent relationship with the volunteer colleague at the office, but it had crossed her mind several times during the day.

Frederik opened the door with a big smile and gave her a big hug and a kiss on her lips. They both felt the emotions running through their minds and did not have words for what was going on between them. Lara could smell his skin and the smell from the kitchen, which had an Italian flavor of spices, tomatoes, and garlic. Frederik took her jacket and held his arm around her as he took her around in his spacious and cozy apartment. The kitchen and living room were one big room, and there was a door leading out to a big balcony overlooking the lake and the central part of the city, which was now full of lights and traffic on the other side and at the end of the lake. The dinner table was already laid with typical Danish table- and stoneware. Frederik had opened an Italian wine from the Chianti wine region and offered Lara a glass. Lara felt very much at home in Frederik's flat since she had lived in homes inspired by and filled with a Nordic design in furniture, art, glassware, and ceramics.

Frederik had cooked an Italian dish consisting of vegetable lasagna with plenty of cheese and served it with a mixed salad. They sat opposite each other and kept direct eye contact throughout the meal. Lara had thought about communicating to Frederik who she was and her expectations of an intimate relationship throughout the day. She had found it difficult to decide which words she would use in this respect. Lara felt it would be fair to Frederik that he knew who he was potentially having an affair with if that was the right word for what was going on between them. She ended up saying that she felt that it was important that they knew more about each other before getting engaged in a more serious relationship. For her part, Frederik needed to know she had had rewarding relationships with both men and women. She believed that people should live in open and equitable relationships with room for other relationships, be it emotional or sexual. She felt that many people locked each other into monogamous relationships, which were too narrow and unrealistic given the nature of human beings. She had never heard from her male and female friends of long-term relationships where one or the other partner had not had affairs outside the relationship. Rather than pretending that you could have a monogamous relationship, she preferred that people were honest with each other and stopped pretending that monogamous relationships existed in real life. She looked at Frederik to assess his reaction to her long monologue about relationships and sensed that he was reflecting on what she had said and was in the process of finding words to respond to her statements. Frederik began by saying that he was not a very sophisticated guy and believed that people should live the lives they could identify with and felt true to themselves as human beings. He, for his part, was heterosexual and had only had sexual relationships with women. He fully agreed with Lara that it was essential to give each other the freedom to explore and develop as a person. Relationships built on social control and fear that the other partner would have affairs with other people would never work in the long run.

Frederik stood up and walked over to Lara's side of the table. He took her hand and led her into the bedroom. They slowly undressed each other without saying a word. Before long, they embraced each other and felt their naked bodies communicating sensually, making them both very excited, tense, and open. Lara could feel how her whole body was opening up to Frederik as she lay down on the bed and felt his hands on her breasts and felt him inside her. She had a climax that was unlike what she had felt for many years, and it gave her a deep feeling of being whole and calm at the same time. They lay together for a long time in a warm, intimate embrace without saying a word.

The next thing Lara experienced was the sound of the early morning traffic. Frederik was lying next to her, and she could feel his warm body radiating an intimacy and calmness, which was very reassuring and created a safe space between them. The events of the past week were on her mind. Lars being critical ill, staying at her childhood home for some days, her relationship with Frederik, and particularly thoughts about what would follow regarding her emotional, family, and working life. She felt it would be best to find a job in another organization if they decided to have a more long-term relationship. Frederik turned around and looked at her with an open, smiling face. They made love again, but this time more slowly, as if their bodies and minds were better connected and more intimately communicated their desire for each other. Frederik looked at his cell phone and realized that it was close to 9 a.m. and that they both had work to do at the office. They grabbed a cup of coffee with some fruit and yogurt before they were walking to the office arm in arm. Lara was still thinking about the implications of this new relationship and asked Frederik if he was ready for another dinner at her apartment the same evening.

Lara's apartment was situated in one of the modern parts of town close to the city center. But the city planners had managed to integrate the new blocks of flats with the old suburban town, which meant that it was not like one of the sterile neighborhoods without any character or atmosphere. The area consisted of a nice mixture of new and long-term residents from all walks of life. Besides, the planners had created a whole new beach park with footbridges, waterways, paths, and access to a long beach with a nice view of the seaway and Southern Sweden on the other side of the sound. Lara had been busy the whole afternoon and early evening preparing for the dinner with Frederik. She had decided to prepare her favorite salmon dish and had bought two bottles of a French white wine she liked and which her parents had served during her upbringing in Geneva. Lara spent a long time looking through her wardrobe to decide what to wear that evening and ended up with a pair of jeans, a colorful blouse, and a scarf her mother had given her the previous week. She was not into make-up but loved to wear a necklace and bracelets. She knew that men were more focused on faces and bodies, whereas women usually knew what other women wore in detail.

Frederik arrived around eight in the evening and had brought one of his small watercolor paintings as a gift. She knew that he was a painter and had seen some of his paintings on previous occasions and appreciated this particular painting from the small town of Skagen on the Northern tip of the mainland. They had a glass of white wine and sat opposite each other in the sofas at the far end of the living room with the view of the sea in the background. They were both aware of the novelty of their love affair and the fact that at a certain level, they knew each other from the two years of working together. Still, at the same time, they had little specific knowledge of each other's families, friends, upbringing, likes, dislikes, milestones, and views on many aspects of life. Lara began by expressing her immediate feelings for Frederik and what she had experienced the last couple of days. She also mentioned that she had had a long chat with her father on the phone that afternoon and that, fortunately, he appeared to be recovering without significant complications. A sound coming from the oven indicated that dinner was ready. Frederik helped bring the food to the table, and they sat down to eat. Frederik enjoyed the food and loved the wine. They were both hungry, and none of them had hardly had any food since breakfast. During the meal, Lara told Frederik that she had applied for a new position in the Danish Foreign Service. They had recently advertised a job in the department responsible for development aid and climate change, and they were looking for a person with Lara's profile. She explained to Frederik that she had been sponsored by the Danish foreign service when she worked for World Health Organization in Geneva and knew several people working in that department. She had already attended one interview and hoped that she would be among the leading candidates for the position. It was clear that Frederik was surprised by this change of events, but he knew that Lara had expressed an interest in international development positions on several occasions.

Frederik looked at her and smiled and said that he would fully support her, and if she needed a reference, he would be more than happy to provide one if need be. They spent the rest of the dinner telling each other more about themselves and bits and pieces of their upbringing, families, and friends. From what Frederik told her about himself, Lara understood why he had become such a calm and warm person. He had had a secure and loving upbringing with both parents' love, tenderness, and care which had not changed after his younger sister was born. His home was in the Northern suburbs of Copenhagen, with lakes, woods, and farmland in the vicinity of his house. Children could safely move around by bicycle, and the many bicycle lanes meant that traffic was not a significant concern for children and their parents. Most of the kids came from well-off, well-functioning families, and they were exposed to the rest of the world through the media, travels, and their schooling. It was given that the children needed a good education and that they had to do some work to supplement the pocket money they received from their parents. All education and health services were free of charge, and parents did not have to take student loans to secure a good education for their children. The tax level was high, but people generally appreciated that they got value for the money they paid to the state and the municipalities. Frederik was a product of the famous Scandinavian welfare state, which had implications for all aspects of life.

Chapter 20

Reality Check

By then, the world was less than ten years from the deadline for reaching the global goal of being carbon neutral in 2050 and preventing temperatures from rising more than 2 degrees Celsius. The average temperature had already risen passed 2 degrees Celsius and was still increasing with predicted catastrophic consequences worldwide. The global sustainability goals had not been reached in 2030, and it had been impossible to set new goals leading up to that year. Low- and middle-income countries had not trusted the high-income countries since they had not fulfilled their obligations under the current agreement and had not provided the assistance needed to mitigate the consequences of the global warming which has already taken place. The United Nations organizations dealing with the increasing number of emergencies were underfunded and had to make unbearable choices due to the lack of funds.

Some success had been accomplished concerning the phasing out of coal used in power generation. Most cars in the Western world and East and Southeast Asia were now battery-powered, substantially reducing air pollution in major cities in those regions of the world. Planes, ships, trucks, and busses were mainly powered by hydrogen. But the countries in South Asia, Africa, and South America were far behind in this transition process. Whereas the power generating sector in the rest of the world was based on renewable energy and nuclear power, these three regions were still relying on fossil fuels for their power generation. The agricultural sector was far behind in meeting its goals worldwide, and people continued to buy and eat too many meat products in middle- and high-income countries. Cement and steel production was still to a large degree based on fossil fuel.

Coastal cities were fighting a losing battle with the rising sea level, and several large cities with millions of inhabitants had already been evacuated. Water was a scarce commodity in Africa, the Middle East, India, China, and North America. The droughts and corresponding wildfires were increasing by the year, leading to even more global warming. The melting tundra in North Asia released vast amounts of methane into the atmosphere and accelerated the planet's warming. There were places in the world that had become uninhabitable since people could no longer work during the day because of the high temperatures. Food and water shortages, rising sea levels, and heat had led to hundreds of millions of refugees in need of support from the national and international community.

A New Beginning

Lara's life changed a lot after she had joined the Danish Foreign Service. She worked in the department dealing with development, climate change, and humanitarian assistance, which allowed her to participate in global, regional, and country-level meetings with participants worldwide. Denmark was one of the leading high-income countries regarding the percentage of the government budget dedicated to development assistance, climate, and humanitarian aid. Most of the assistance was channeled through the United Nations, the European Commission, Global and Regional Funds and Banks, and national and international non-governmental organizations. The remaining aid was retained in the Foreign Service for special initiatives, which required a high degree of flexibility in using the funds. Most of the work was carried out online in conference calls with the collaborating partners. But it also involved traveling for meetings and supervision of the use of Danish aid worldwide. Lara often thought of the work her father had carried out when he had worked in the Foreign Service and as a volunteer more than 30 years ago. From a situation where almost all high-income countries had separate funding for programs and projects in the recipient countries to the present time, where developing countries were funded through general budget support or dedicated global and regional funds for specific sectors such as education and health. Lara was in the section monitoring the aid going to countries in Eastern and Southern Africa. The challenges were daunting given the increasing climate-related emergencies and the number of low-income countries unable to cope with even the basic needs of their populations in the form of shelter, food, water, power, schooling, health, and infrastructure. Internally displaced people constituted an increasing challenge in many countries, including refugees crossing borders to escape the worst effects of the rising political, security, and climate-related emergencies. These challenges called for a robust response from the international community and close coordination between all the agencies involved. Lara loved her work in the foreign service and felt in a way that her whole life, upbringing, education, and work experiences had prepared her for this assignment.

The work was more or less a 24/7 assignment which did not leave much time for other activities in her life. Besides her work, she spent most of her free time with Frederik and her Danish family. She occasionally visited her parents in Geneva and was particularly relieved that her father was slowly but steadily improving after his skiing accident. She and Frederik still kept their respective apartments, but they were increasingly spending their lives together at either her or his place. They occasionally had the opportunity to travel together and spent most of their holidays in the Mediterranean countries.

Given Lara's working experience with Unicef and the World Health Organization, she was the focal point in her section when meetings were held with the two organizations and the Global Health Fund. The latter had been established to assist countries in strengthening the capacity of their health sectors to deliver quality essential health services and allow them to purchase high-cost equipment, medicine, and vaccines for their populations. In this capacity, Lara participated in a review mission to Tanzania to assess the Global Health Funds support utilization. It was her first visit to Tanzania in many years, but her upbringing in Dar es Salaam was still remarkably close to her heart. The trip took her to the Morogoro Region, where they stayed a few nights at the Mikumi National Park. She loved Mikumi, which she had visited many times as a child. It had been her first encounter with wildlife in Africa, and Mikumi was unique with its high concentration of elephants, giraffes, zebras, wildebeest, hippos, hyenas, and lions, and spectacular birdlife. During the night, she loved listening to the sound of hyenas and lions that often came very close to the tented camp in Mikumi.

They visited the Morogoro Regional Government Hospital to see with their own eyes what difference the aid made to childcare in the region. The ward for malnourished children was a unique experience for the review team and, in particular, for the women on the team. Malnutrition was still a significant problem in Tanzania, and it had recently increased due to the frequency and severity of the droughts and flooding in the area. Some of the children in the ward were recovering and looked relatively healthy. A girl around the age of three had come up to Lara and hugged her during the visit. It was only later that Lara realized that something had happened that day at the hospital. For most of her life, she had considered having children as something that concerned other women. She had occasionally acknowledged that she would like to have children one day but the little girl that day changed something in her body and mind.

She had a growing feeling that she would like to become a mother and have a child.

Sara

Lara's encounter with the little girl in Tanzania had given her life a new dimension. She had been unable to provide a rational explanation to her current deep-felt urge to have her own child. She felt that her normally rational personality had been put on standby and overtaken by more vital forces that were outside her control. She had tried to explain her feelings to Frederik, and he had been very understanding but could not follow her emotional transition and the wish to have a child. They had known each other for almost four years by then and were both in their mid-thirties. It was clear that Frederik was ready to take responsibility for a child at one level, but on the other hand, he knew that it would be a significant change in their relationship and a commitment for the rest of their lives.

Lara got pregnant a few months after having her IUD removed. That started a new phase of her life that changed both physically and emotionally, which she had never been able to imagine. She increasingly saw her life divided into two phases, before and after becoming pregnant. Frederik had been doing his best to follow Lara in her pregnancy but quickly realized that there were many aspects in the process he could not understand as a man. Frederik had learned that having children was not a private matter but an event that had deep roots in human history and the survival of the family, clan, and society. From being an induvial person with the perception that he could control his life, he felt that that phase of his life had come to its natural conclusion.

Lara's parents had been very excited about Lara's pregnancy and the prospect of becoming grandparents. It would be Carole's first grandchild, and Lara's pregnancy had set in motion numerous feelings and thoughts about her role concerning Lara's pregnancy and the baby. Lars had been a grandfather for many years, but Lara was very special to him. He had not had extensive contact with his other grandchildren but expected to have a closer relationship with Lara's child. Fortunately, Lars was recovering from his skiing accident some years back, and he and Carole had been visiting Lara regularly in Copenhagen during the pregnancy.

Lara gave birth to a healthy girl at the age of 35 and had one year's maternity leave to ensure that her child, Sara, got the best start in life. During her maternity leave, Lara applied and was accepted for a position at the Danish UN Mission in Geneva beginning the following year. Frederik had the opportunity to join the European headquarters for the international organization he was representing in Denmark. By the end of that year, the little family moved to Geneva, where they managed to rent a house close to where Lars and Carole were living. It would make it possible for her parents to take care of Sara when Lara or Frederik was busy traveling in their respective jobs.

Lars helped Lara and Frederik with many administrative and practical matters associated with moving into a new house. Lars had noticed over the last couple of years that even though he was now in his late seventies, it was as if his aging process had slowed down, and he was still able to do things that most of his friends had stopped doing. Lars was aware that he had lived a healthy life for most of his life, eaten a healthy balanced diet, and had exercised consistently. Carole was still very fit for her age and was able to assist Lara and Frederik with the day-to-day care for Sara and enjoyed the experience of caring for a baby again. However, she was more aware of the aging processes and had the impression that women were aging faster than men at her age.

Chapter 23

Point of No Return

For decades, the people living on Earth had been told that the world was rapidly moving towards a situation where climate changes would become irreversible and create feedback mechanisms accelerating the buildup of CO_2 in the atmosphere, thereby leading to increased global warming. Although a growing number of carbon capture systems had been taking CO_2 out of the atmosphere for some time, they could not keep up with the increasing amount of CO_2 in the atmosphere. So far, global warming had created seasonal heath waves and bush fires. Still, this year more and more places on Earth were experiencing a climate that led to continuous drought and heatwave situations. To make matters worse, the tundra in Northern Asia and America was disappearing at an alarming rate leading to the emission of methane which had been trapped in the tundra for thousands of years. The financial-, pension- and insurance sectors were beginning to experience the challenges associated with abandoned cities, investment returns crumbling, and an increasing number of claims that the insurance market had struggled to honor. The very fabric of modern society had come under severe stress affecting everyone and lead to the erratic behavior of individuals, companies, organizations, governments, and international institutions. Many people were aware of what was going on but felt helpless about dealing with the problem and expected their respective governments to deal with it. Populism had been on the increase for many years, but in the last decade, more and more countries were led by populist governments that had promised their respective citizens that they would solve the problems at hand. Again, this meant that the international institutions charged with addressing the global warming problems were increasingly blocked from doing their business, either because of lack of funds or because the populist governments paralyzed their governing bodies.

The rapid climate changes and the associated socioeconomic challenges had set in motion a mass exodus in parts of the western world unseen in modern time. Many people were leaving the Western and Southern parts of the United States, heading mainly for the states on the Northeastern seaboard but inland away from the rising sea. In Europe, many people were moving away from the Mediterranean areas towards the Central and Northern parts of Europe. Countries like Australia, Canada, and New Zealand saw a marked increase in people seeking to move to the three countries.

Chapter 24

Working Against the Clock

At the Danish Mission in Geneva, Lara was responsible for the Danish support to the World Health Organization and the Global Health Fund. Both organizations were in crisis mode, trying to respond to the global health and humanitarian crises. She attended many of the ongoing emergency meetings dealing with all countries, regions, and continents of the world, including the large refugee camps in Southern Europe housing millions of refugees from Africa and the Middle East. Geneva and Switzerland, in general, were still functioning reasonably well with no essential shortages and few signs of the world spiraling out of control. The contrast between Lara's daily work and her time at home with Sara, Frederik, and her parents became surreal in many respects. Their discussions focused increasingly on what they should do as individuals in the situation currently unfolding around them. Lara and Frederik found it increasingly difficult to imagine the kind of life Sara would have in the future. They were both dedicating their working life to addressing the challenges and effects of global warming, but both felt that it looked increasingly as if the world had done too little too late. The hope they both had had that it would be possible to avert the rising temperatures and mitigate the worst effects of the increasing temperatures was slowly evaporating and replaced by fear for the future and anxiousness for their wellbeing and the future of their child.

Countries were increasingly fighting for survival and taking steps that were not in the world community's interest. It had the effect of undermining the world economy and the flow of food and goods, including lifesaving medicines, vaccines, and medical equipment. Travel between countries was restricted by rules put in place by individual countries, making it harder to share the burden of the many internally and externally displaced people and refugees. Regional conflicts over access to water were making the crisis even more challenging, and the remaining superpowers were not engaging in the solution of these conflicts but spent all resources addressing the evolving turmoil in their home countries.

Epilogue

The above scenario is not inevitable, but it will take all of us to prevent it from happening. Titanic is still on course to hit the iceberg, but we still have time to steer past it if we focus the next ten to twenty years on implementing the necessary preventive and mitigating measures. If we wait much longer, our children and grandchildren will share their fate with Lara, Sara, and Frederik.